For Kim, Davina and Paul Holness,
and Ted Silva in America

Originally published in Great Britain in 1992 by ABC, All Books for
Children, a division of The All Children's Company Ltd.

Copyright © 1992 by Peter O'Donnell.
All rights reserved. Published by Scholastic Inc.,
730 Broadway, New York, NY 10003, by arrangement with
ABC, All Books for Children, a division of
The All Children's Company Ltd.

Library of Congress Cataloging-in-Publication Data
O'Donnell, Peter.
Carnegie's excuse / Peter O'Donnell.
p.   cm.
Summary: Carnegie explains why she's late for school — a tiger jumped in her window.
ISBN 0-590-46435-3
[1. Homework — Fiction. 2. Tigers — Fiction.
3. Animals — Fiction. 4. Amusement parks — Fiction.] I. Title.
PZ7.02245Car   1993
[E] — dc20   92-17617
                                             CIP
                                              AC

12 11 10 9 8 7 6 5 4 3 2 1   3 4 5 6 7 8/9
Printed in Hong Kong
First Scholastic printing, May 1993

Carnegie's Excuse

Peter O'Donnell

SCHOLASTIC INC. · NEW YORK

Carnegie was late for school. Again.
"Carnegie," said her teacher. "What
is it this time?"
Carnegie took a deep breath. Then
she began her story.

"Last night a tiger leaped right through our window. He couldn't find the amusement park and wanted to ask the tiger on our TV for directions.

"I offered to show him the way."

"So we started out. I had
to hold on tight, because
he could jump so high."

"Then we decided to row across the water.
"A big blue shark said he'd come with
us as far as the other side."

"When we got to shore,
I felt sorry for the shark. He
couldn't go on, because he
couldn't walk. So I got a
shopping cart and pushed him.
   "Finally we reached the park.
A gorilla was learning to drive
by reading a book while
practicing on the bumper cars.
   "He wasn't doing very well."

"I helped out by reading the book to the gorilla. Soon he was scooting in and out."

"When it was time to go, he rented a car and drove us all to my house."

"We sneaked in. I told everyone to be quiet, so I could go to sleep. I didn't want to be late for school in the morning."

"But I overslept this morning, because we were out so late. Then I couldn't find my book, because the gorilla had been reading it.

"That's why I'm late this morning."

"I'm sorry."
Carnegie's teacher looked at her.
Her classmates looked at her.

"Carnegie. Your imagination is bigger than
you are. You will stay after school today."
When Carnegie finally left school that afternoon,
her new friends were waiting to take her home.

They couldn't understand
why no one believed her and
cheered her up by drawing
funny pictures of each other.

The next morning,
Carnegie got up extra
early. The tiger got
up and said it was
time for him to go back
to the jungle. The shark
decided to go back to
the water. The gorilla
thought he'd drive around
for a while.

They took Carnegie
to school. She said good-bye
to them and good morning
to her teacher.

Carnegie *never* had to
stay after school again.